Dear Parent:
Your child's love of reading starts here!

Every child learns to read in a different way and at his or her own speed. Some go back and forth between reading levels and read favorite books again and again. Others read through each level in order. You can help your young reader improve and become more confident by encouraging his or her own interests and abilities. From books your child reads with you to the first books he or she reads alone, there are I Can Read Books for every stage of reading:

SHARED READING
Basic language, word repetition, and whimsical illustrations, ideal for sharing with your emergent reader

BEGINNING READING
Short sentences, familiar words, and simple concepts for children eager to read on their own

READING WITH HELP
Engaging stories, longer sentences, and language play for developing readers

READING ALONE
Complex plots, challenging vocabulary, and high-interest topics for the independent reader

ADVANCED READING
Short paragraphs, chapters, and exciting themes for the perfect bridge to chapter books

I Can Read Books have introduced children to the joy of reading since 1957. Featuring award-winning authors and illustrators and a fabulous cast of beloved characters, I Can Read Books set the standard for beginning readers.

A lifetime of discovery begins with the magical words "I Can Read!"

Visit www.icanread.com for information
on enriching your child's reading experience.

Library of Congress catalog card number: 2012938598
ISBN 978-0-06-211067-1 (trade bdg.) – ISBN 978-0-06-211066-4 (pbk.)

13 14 15 16 LP/WOR   10 9 8 7 6 5 4 3 2   ❖   First Edition

Pete the Cat

PLAY BALL!

created by James Dean

HARPER

An Imprint of HarperCollinsPublishers

4

Here comes Pete the Cat.

Pete has a mitt.

He has a bat and a ball.

What will Pete do today?

Pete will play baseball!

Today is the big game.

The Rocks are playing the Rolls.

Pete and his team get set.

They play catch.

They take turns hitting.

It is time to play ball!

The Rocks bat first.
Pete waits for his turn.

9

Crack! The batter hits the ball.

He runs to first base.

"Way to go!" Pete cheers.

"Batter up!" says the umpire.
Pete goes up to bat.

The pitcher throws the ball.

Pete swings the bat.

He misses the ball.

Strike one!

The pitcher pitches again.
Pete swings too high.
Strike two!

The pitcher winds up.

He throws.

Pete strikes out.

But Pete is not sad.

He did his best.

Pete's friend Ben is up.

Ben hits a home run!

"Way to go!" cheers Pete.

The Rolls go up to bat.

The Rocks go to the field.

Crack! Here comes a fly ball!

"I've got it!" calls Pete.

The ball hits his mitt.

But Pete drops it.

He is not sad.

He did his best.

Another hit!

This time Pete catches it,

but he throws it too far.

Pete is up at bat again.

He wants to hit the ball.

The first pitch is too low.

Pete does not swing.

Ball one!

The next pitch is too high.

Pete does not swing.

Ball two!

The third pitch is inside.

The fourth pitch is outside.

Pete gets four balls.

Pete wanted to get a hit.

But a walk is cool, too.

The next batter gets a hit.

Pete runs as fast as he can.

Pete wants to score,

but he is out at home plate.

Pete is not sad.

He did his best.

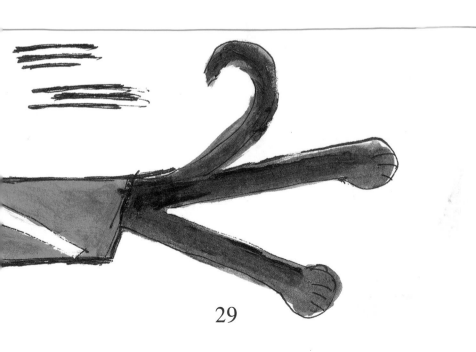

The game is over.

The Rocks win six to three!

"Way to go!" calls Pete.

"Good game," the Rocks say.

"Good game," the Rolls say.

Pete did his best.

He had fun.

What a great game!